DOUBLE TROUBLE

Adapted by Kate Howard

SCHOLASTIC INC.

LEGO, the LEGO logo, NEXO KNIGHTS, the NEXO KNIGHTS logo, the Brick and Knob configurations and the Minifigure are trademarks of/ sont des marques de commerce du the LEGO Group. © 2016 The LEGO Group. All rights reserved. Produced by Scholastic Inc. under license from the LEGO Group.

Published by Scholastic Inc., *Publishers since 1920.* SCHOLASTIC and associated logos are trademarks and/or registered trademarks of Scholastic Inc.

ISBN 978-1-338-03803-3

10 9 8 7 6 5 4 3 2 1   16 17 18 19 20

Printed in the U.S.A.   40
First printing, 2016
Book design by Rick DeMonico

CONTENTS

FROM THE
FILES OF
MERLOK 2.0

Greetings and welcome to the files of Merlok 2.0—that's me! Now where was I . . . ah, yes! For over one hundred years, the kingdom of Knighton knew only peace. Nothing threatened the beautiful Realm, and so the people there were able to create amazing technology. In the capital city of Knightonia, humans and Squirebots began to live side by side, surrounded by the city's technical marvels—like the awe-inspiring Beam Bridges or the state-of-the-art Joustdome.

I, Merlok the wizard, used my magic to help the kingdom whenever I could. My greatest task was to keep the dangerous Books of Dark Magic locked away in my library. The most wicked of these books was The Book of Monsters. Under my very nose, this clever book plotted to escape from my library.

One day, the book found the perfect puppet for its plans: Jestro, the court jester. Jestro had no friends in the kingdom except for Clay Moorington. Clay tried to be kind to the jester, but everyone else thought Jestro was a joke—and not the funny kind. Jestro was tired of everyone laughing at him instead of with him.

Lonely and eager to prove that he was nothing to be laughed at, Jestro was a perfect target for The Book of Monsters' offer. If Jestro freed it, together they could unleash evil on Knighton. Soon, the citizens of Knighton would be serving Jestro, not laughing at him.

Jestro and The Book of Monsters launched their attack right away. With a wave of a magic staff over the pages of The Book of Monsters, evil monsters sprang to life.

A team of brave knights banded together to fight them. Clay Moorington and his friends Lance Richmond, Macy Halbert, Aaron Fox, and Axl took up their shields and charged against the monsters. But muscle and iron are no match against magic monsters.

In the end, I was the only one who could stop them. I cast a powerful magic spell to destroy the monsters and . . . *boom!* Jestro and The Book of Monsters were blown far away from the castle. Although the monsters were defeated, my library was also destroyed, and dangerous Books of Dark Magic were scattered across the kingdom.

The explosion also left me trapped as a digital hologram in the castle's computer system. But it isn't all bad. Now I am able to harness the power of magic and technology together. In this new form I can download magical NEXO Powers to the knights, so they can defeat whatever monsters attack.

Now it's a fair fight. Clay, Lance, Macy, Aaron, and Axl train with their upgraded weapons, vehices, and armor so they'll always be ready when Jestro and The Book of Monsters attack—and those troublemakers will! The NEXO KNIGHTS team has only just begun to see what Jestro's monsters can do.

Now the sneaky jester has found a copy of one of the lost Books of Dark Magic—the devious *Book of Deception*. But what mischief will Jestro unleash with his new prize? Only time will tell . . .

CHAPTER 1

Ha! I still can't believe we got away with The Book of Deception and totally faked out the knights! I feel so, so successful!" Jestro giggled, holding his prize high as he stood atop the hulking Evil Mobile.

The devious court jester and his even *more* devious sidekick, The Book of Monsters, were on a quest around the Realm. Their goal was to find and collect magical books with evil beasts and cruel spells trapped inside. Once they found them, they could use them to terrorize all the people of Knighton.

The only thing that was slowing Jestro

and The Book of Monsters down on their quest for destruction and doom was a pack of interfering, fresh-out-of-training knights. Jestro thought the NEXO KNIGHTS team was stubborn and stuck-up. And their mission to help bring peace and safety to the people of the Realm made him sick. Ruling through evil, he thought, was way more fun than all this goody-goody knight stuff. Sure, the NEXO Powers the knights could download from their wizard's operating system were cool— but his Book of Monsters was even more amazing and powerful!

In fact, The Book of Monsters was a very unusual and important sidekick. Without the book, Jestro would just be a failed jester with a chip on his shoulder. But *with* The Book of Monsters in his possession, Jestro was incredibly powerful. For every time Jestro found one of the magical books hidden around the Realm, he would feed it to The Book of Monsters—and a moment later, the creatures and powers that had been stuck between the pages of the evil book would come to life. This little trick was great for Jestro, and not-so-great for the rest of Knighton.

Jestro just *loved* having so much control over evil! Now he rubbed his new prize lovingly, gazing at the beautiful Book of Deception in his arms. What kind of fun, new tricks could he unlock with this magical treasure? He couldn't wait to feed it to his sidekick and find out!

"Yeah, but it's a tricky book," The Book of Monsters reminded him. The Book of Monsters—who was, yes, an actual talking book—knew that most of the magical books hidden throughout Knighton were filled with danger that had to be carefully managed. Jestro rarely took his sidekick's advice, but The Book of Monsters always tried to warn him anyway. It was fun to say "I told you so" later.

The Book of Monsters tried again: "You gotta stop foolin' around with it or—"

Pop! The Book of Monsters and Jestro both jumped. Suddenly, a second copy of The Book of Deception appeared out of nowhere. *Pop!* A third copy, then a fourth, and a fifth. *Pop! Pop! Pop! Pop!* Within seconds, there were hundreds of copies of The Book of Deception stacked up all around the Evil Mobile.

"What is going on?!" Jestro shrieked.

"I just told you." The Book of Monsters sighed. "That's its thing. It makes copies of itself to be deceptive. Just feed me the real deal already and let's be done with it." The Book of Monsters opened his mouth wide, waiting.

"Right . . ." Jestro said, staring at all the books piled up around him. He scratched the blue-and-red jester hat perched on top of his head. He plucked a book off the top of one of the stacks. "Okay, well, I guess I have to just keep feeding you until we find the right one."

"No, wait—we should put—" The Book of Monsters began. But Jestro stuffed the book into his sidekick's mouth before he could say anything more. The Book of Monsters chewed the pages up, his reddish-orange eyes glowing. He munched and chomped, devouring the book as fast as possible. But it was just a useless copy of The Book of Deception, so nothing happened.

Jestro tried feeding his partner another book, and another—tossing them as quickly as possible into The Book of Monster's mouth. None were the real thing. All through the night, Jestro stuffed book after book into The Book of Monsters' mouth, searching for the one with magical powers. But every time he failed to find the real book, he grew more and more frustrated. He was desperate to find the one that would unlock more evil powers! He was ready to do some damage!

By the time dawn broke, there were only a few books left scattered around the Evil Mobile. The forest around the huge vehicle began to come to life as creatures woke for the day. The Book of Monsters kept chewing until, finally, Jestro held up the very last book. He waved it in the air and said, "Well, this is the last one. It better be the real deal."

The Book of Monsters licked his dry and papery mouth. "Uh, yeah. Because I can't handle any more empty calories."

Jestro tossed the last copy of the book through the air. It arced high, then tumbled down into The Book of Monsters' waiting chompers. He gulped it down. "Mmmm, delicious!" He burped out a thick cloud of purple smoke—this was what Jestro had been waiting for. Magical purple smoke was the telltale sign that they had finally found the trapped magic. "But these books are deceptively high in calories. I must weigh a ton."

The Bookkeeper, who was charged with

toting The Book of Monsters around, peered around the book's cover and nodded. Then he collapsed under the weight of the heavy book.

The Book of Monsters chuckled and cried out, "Okay, let's go do some deceiving!"

Elsewhere in Knighton, the NEXO KNIGHTS team was ready for its next brave quest. The knights' rolling castle, called the Fortrex, rumbled across the countryside.

"*Da-da-da-daaaaaa!*" Inside the castle's command center, Merlok 2.0 tried to make himself sound like a royal bugle to get the knights' attention. Even though he was nothing more than a bright orange hologram, the knights' mentor had some pretty cool magic at his disposal. Merlok 2.0 could download weapons the knights required straight to them, whenever they needed help during a battle.

Merlok 2.0 tooted his horn sound again, but no one came running. "My, my," he said, scratching his digital beard. "There must be an easier way to get everyone's attention . . ." He tooted again.

Suddenly, Robin Underwood ran breathlessly into the room. Robin was one of the knights' helpers, and a student at the Knights' Academy. He slid into his seat in front of the computer and punched at the keyboard.

"Whoa!" Robin said, panting. "Check it out! Energy readings are off the charts. We're tracking something big!" He leapt to his feet and ran toward the door again. Robin couldn't wait to set a plan in action! Someone in Knighton was up to no good, and this was his chance to help the knights save the day!

On his way out of the command center, Robin bumped into Axl, the largest of the knights. Axl giggled when Robin bounced off his enormous armored chest.

The other four knights fanned out beside Axl, forming a wall that kept Robin from going anywhere.

"Uh, Robin," Clay Moorington said gently, looking down at the eager knight-in-training. Clay was a big believer in there being a right time and place for everything—and he knew Robin had a ways to go before he was ready to get in on the knights' heroics. "I know you want to help, but don't you have to get back to the Knights' Academy for the new semester?"

"Aww," Robin whined. "But I don't like school! I'm a doer, not a studier. Just check out what I can do!" Robin grabbed a Squirebot and began to rewire it. He fiddled with a bunch of wires, reprogramming the robot to do exactly what he wanted it to. Suddenly, the Squirebot began to tap dance.

Clay, Axl, and the other knights clapped along to the music.

"Pretty awesome, huh?" Robin said, beaming. "Those kind of tech skills should make up for any lack of formal training, right?"

Wrong.

Moments later, the Fortrex rolled up in front of the Knights' Academy and Robin rolled out. He stood sadly in front of the school gates, beside his classmate Ava Prentis. Ava, a computer genius, was Merlok 2.0's tech apprentice. But she, too, was still in school and had to return to the Academy for the new semester of classes. "Nice try, Robin," Ava said, shrugging. She and Robin both watched the knights' rolling Fortex zoom away. "But it'll take a lot more than a tap-dancing Squirebot to get you out of school."

Robin knew that. He also knew he wasn't going to let school stop him from proving he had what it took to be a knight. He was sure he could show the rest of the knights and Merlok 2.0 that he belonged on the front lines—somehow!

CHAPTER 2

Just moments after they dropped Robin and Ava off at school, the five knights marched into the village of Appleton— hundreds of miles away. Close observers would have wondered how the group could have traveled such a distance in such a short amount of time.

As they made their way into the town's square, the knights looked bold and power- ful in their armor. The team's unofficial leader, Clay Moorington, took his place at the center of the pack. He puffed out his chest under his blue and silver armor, making himself look as heroic as possible. Even though he— like the others—was a recent graduate of the Knights' Academy, Clay prided himself on his extreme knightliness.

On one side of Clay, Macy Halbert—a princess who did *not* like when people told her she fought like a girl—stormed into town, ready to prove herself.

On Clay's other side, Axl—the huge, always-hungry member of their team—flexed his enormous muscles.

Lance Richmond stood on one end of the group, wearing his flashy silver armor. Lance usually liked to be as close as possible to the crowds of people who came out to adore and admire him. He was the most famous of the knights—and he took great pride in being noticed.

Aaron Fox flanked the group on the other side of the line of knights. The most daring one on the team, Aaron usually preferred to make a more dramatic entrance—on his hover shield—but today he was simply marching into town with the rest of the knights.

The villagers in Appleton lined the streets to cheer for the heroes.

"Welcome, brave knights!" they called out. The townsfolk rang bells, threw flowers, and waved banners in the air—banners filled with pictures of the knights.

Suddenly, Clay growled and tossed his sword through the air. The sharp blade cracked a banner's pole in half. The waving fabric fell to the ground. Clay stepped forward and stomped on the banner, crushing it into the dirt.

A moment later, a villager threw a bouquet of flowers at Macy. Macy squeezed the stems, then tossed them back in the woman's face, knocking her to the ground.

Overhead, a majestic bell rang over and over again—announcing the knights' arrival. With a sneer, Aaron fired his bow and released an arrow. The arrow sliced through the bell's rope and the enormous bell crashed down to the bottom of the bell tower.

Further along the town's main street, a sweet young boy held up a framed picture of Lance, begging the famous knight to autograph it for him. Lance grabbed the photo and carelessly hurled it at the boy. The boy shrieked and jumped out of the way. The photo crashed into a wall, scattering glass everywhere. The little boy sobbed, brokenhearted.

"Hey!" one of the townspeople shouted, waving his fist as he approached the knights. "Stop that, Sir Knight! You're being rude!"

In response, Axl reached over and swept the villager off the ground. Then he tossed him into a cart of apples. The people of Appleton stared, horrified. The NEXO KNIGHTS heroes weren't usually like this. Usually, they were kind and thoughtful, looking out for the people of Knighton.

But now the knights just laughed and chased the townsfolk out of the center square. People screamed as the knights chased them down. The five usually-kind knights growled and attacked, pillaging the town. They overturned market stalls, sent barrels tumbling, broke windows, and stole valuables from every person they came across. The townsfolk scattered and fled as the knights filled sacks with jewels and other stolen goods. Then they strutted out of town, leaving the people of Appleton to wonder what on earth had happened to their heroes.

Later that night, on the other side of the Realm, Robin was trying to settle back into the Academy by watching a little Holovision. Suddenly, he sat up straight and gasped, "No way! Did you see *that*?"

Ava stepped into the Holovision room and stared up at the screen. She read the headline flashing across the news screen. "Good Knights Gone Bad?!"

Reporter Alice Squires was on screen. She shook her head and announced, "For the second time today, the *saviors* of our Realm are *savaging* one of its villages. This time, they're attacking Boork, renowned kingdom-wide for its delicious bacon-wrapped pork fritters. Yum!" The reporter held up a fritter, ready to take a bite. But before she got a taste, an angry Axl roared and grabbed it out of her hand. Then he threw the fritter to the ground and stomped on it like a bug.

"What happened to our knights?" Ava asked, staring in shock at the television screen.

"I dunno," Robin said, shrugging in disbelief. He watched footage of the knights destroying the village and attacking its people. He looked at Ava with a concerned expression on his face. "But who's gonna stand up for Knighton now?"

CHAPTER 3

W hoa..." Macy said later that night. She scanned the massive destruction in the village of Appleton, horrified by the damage. The knights had just arrived there from Boork. "What kind of hideous brutes did this?"

Clay shook his head. Speaking loudly, he announced, "We must let these good people know they're under *our* protection now."

A lone apple flew through the air and conked Clay's helmet with a *ping*! "We don't *want* your protection!" one of the villagers yelled.

"What?" Clay gasped, astonished. In the short time he and the other knights had been protecting the Realm, they had found that they were always warmly welcomed in the villages they visited. The people were grateful for their protection, and usually greeted them with bells, cheering, and a warm meal. Clay was stumped ... why were the people of Appleton suddenly acting so different?

Another villager screamed out, "See what happened the last time you 'protected' us?" He gestured at the mess that filled the town square. "Get lost!"

Lance held up a hand, smiling serenely. "Perhaps you misunderstood ..." He winked. "We're your *heroes*! Observe." He struck an over-the-top hero pose. His pearly-white teeth sparkled in the moonlight. But his smile quickly faded when the villagers gathered in the town square began pelting the group with apples.

The five knights turned their vehicles and fled as a shower of apples and pork fritters rained down on them. They blasted their way through the town, dodging the food attack.

"Well, *that* has never happened before," Lance said, his eyes wide with disbelief.

"C'mon, Clay," Aaron shouted from his hover shield. "We can take 'em!"

Clay shook his head. "No. We are not fighting a bunch of innocent villagers!"

"But they threw apples at me!" Axl whined, ducking his head to avoid another round of tasty missiles. Something warm and salty bounced off his helmet. Axl lifted it to his nose and sniffed, curious. "And bacon-wrapped pork fritters?" He took a bite and cheered up a bit. "Yum! They attack with mouth-watering comfort food!"

On the far end of town, Lance slowed his vehicle when he saw a young boy holding up a framed picture. The boy waved it in the air, trying to get Lance's attention.

"Ah!" Lance said, beaming. "Now that's

more like it. A member of my adoring public, seeking an autograph. Let me help you there, young fan of mine." He reached forward, happily bending down to sign the photo. But as he did, the boy tossed the picture at Lance's head, narrowly missing him.

"Eek!" Lance shrieked. "That is so rude!"

The knights raced out of town while villagers continued to attack them. As soon as they reached the outskirts of the village, the five knights slowed and looked back. Clay turned to the others and asked, "Just what is going on here?!"

Deep in the forest, the evil "knights" were celebrating their successful day of looting and pillaging from unsuspecting citizens. Each of the "knights" carried its loot through the woods until they came upon their leader: Jestro. As the scheming team approached Jestro, he jumped up and screamed. "Ahhh!" he cried. "It's those do-gooder knights!"

Jestro spun around and ran toward a path, hurrying to get away. But instead of leading toward safety, the path dead-ended in a slab of painted—and painful—steel. Jestro slammed into the make-believe path and crumpled to the ground. "Lemme guess," Jestro said, rubbing his head. "Another 'trick' from The Book of Deception?"

The Book of Monsters chuckled and said, "Its powers are so magically misleading! That's actually a solid wall of steel, designed to *look* like an escape path." The painted wall fell over, crashing into the ground with a magnificent *thud*! "All part of the power that helped us create those fake 'knights' over there." The Book of Monsters swiveled around, watching as the five knights were surrounded by a purple swirl of magic smoke.

A moment later, the fake Clay, Lance, Aaron, Axl, and Macy turned back into Moltor, Flama, Sparkks, Burnzie, and Lavaria. Some of Jestro's evil henchmen had posed as the knights in order to spread terror across Knighton. Jestro cheered. This new magic of deception was genius! His evil henchmen, pretending to be fake knights? This was extraordinary!

The Book of Monsters smiled. "Now comes my favorite part!"

Jestro cheered even louder when his Evil Mobile transformed into an exact replica of the knights' rolling Fortrex. "Ooh! Ooh! You could make two of *me*," Jestro said, whooping. "Then I could be twice as evil!"

The Book of Monsters rolled its eyes. "Or twice as much of a pain in my back cover. Let's just stick to *this* plan first."

CHAPTER 4

Many miles away, the real Fortrex rolled merrily across the country-side. But inside the enormous moving castle, the NEXO KNIGHTS team was far from merry. They were wiping apple guts and bacon grease off their weapons and armor when a royal trumpet fanfare blasted through the armory room. The view-screen flashed and came to life.

"Ah!" Clay said, brightening. "Royal chain mail from King Halbert. Maybe *he* can tell us why everyone's so angry at us all of a sudden."

The king appeared on the view-screen. The scowl on his usually cheerful face told

28

them all that their royal ruler was *not* happy. "Knights!" the king's message began. "Have you gone mad?"

Clay glanced at the others. They all shared a look of confusion. "Huh?" Clay wondered.

"What are you doing to my kingdom?" the message went on.

"Us?" Axl asked, even though the king couldn't hear him. "But—"

He was cut off as the king ranted, "I've received *terrible* reports from the villages of Appleton and Boork!"

"No kidding," Aaron said quietly. "Those places were trashed!"

"Those places were trashed!" King Halbert echoed.

Aaron smirked. "Told ya."

"And the villagers blame *you*!" the king screamed.

"What?!" Lance gasped.

King Halbert shook his finger at the screen and went on, "You are supposed to be this

Kingdom's NEXO KNIGHTS heroes! And Macy, you're our princess! Is this any way to behave?"

Macy sputtered, "Well, no, of course not. But, Dad—"

"I want an explanation!" the king cried. "Or I'm shutting you and your rolling castle down. King Halbert *out*!" The view-screen flickered off.

The five knights exchanged puzzled looks. "Can he really do that?" Lance wondered aloud.

"No," Clay assured him. "But Ava and Robin probably can. Whoever is out there spreading these rumors about us, and attacking these towns … we knights must stop them!"

Not so far away, Jestro and his crew of evildoers were continuing on their path of terror and destruction. "Village ahead!" Lavaria cried, pointing at a town on the top of a high hill. She and the other fake "knights" were ready to don their disguises again and trash another town. "Knight up!"

The haze of purple smoke surrounded the five fiery creatures, magically turning them into the five imposter knights once again. The Evil Mobile—now magically disguised as the Fortrex—lumbered up the hill toward the village of Hightop. The castle ground to a halt just before reaching the outskirts of the town.

"Wait!" Moltor—who was disguised as Clay—growled. Something was standing in the road, blocking the castle from cresting the hill. "Is that a Black Knight?"

A huge, black mech stood between the people of Hightop and Jestro's crew. "None shall pass!" the enormous protector said in a deep, booming voice.

Moltor narrowed his eyes. He shouted, "Look: We've got no beef with you, Black Knight. So step aside!"

The Black Knight didn't budge. Once again, the giant protector boomed out, "None shall pass."

Lavaria—pretending to be Macy—sneered, "Well, the 'good knights' will just have to teach him a lesson!"

The drawbridge on the rolling castle dropped open and Jestro's team of bad guys—still disguised as the knights—charged toward the Black Knight. They were ready for battle! But the Black Knight didn't seem concerned. He didn't move. Rather, he towered over the team of evildoers, looking menacing.

"Go away, Black Knight!" Moltor growled. "If anyone raids that town, it's gonna be us."

Lavaria nudged him in the ribs. "Uh-oh," she said, nodding her head toward a crowd of villagers. The people of Hightop were watching the face off between the knights and the Black Knight with great interest. "Townsfolk watching. If we want to keep up this ruse, you need to sound a *lot* more like 'Clay.'"

"What?" Moltor grumbled. "How do I do that?"

Lavaria shrugged. "Try saying something a little more goofy and self-righteous."

"Oh, yeah," Moltor said, smirking. "So, uh . . ." He cleared his throat, trying to mimic Clay's voice. He boomed, "We are knights! We are shiny! And, uh . . . you are not!"

The Black Knight said nothing, just stared down at the five imposters through glowing yellow eyes.

Moltor glanced at Lavaria, who nodded her approval. "Not bad," she told him. "Add some blah-blah about justice, courage, and chivalry."

Moltor puffed out his chest and added, "So, uh . . . we fight for juicebox! And curry! And shiver-me-timbers!" He shook his fist, then pulled out his sword. He charged toward the Black Knight and screamed, "And now we attack, as I cry *blah-blah-blah*!"

The three other "knights" echoed his cry—"*Blah-blah-blah!*"—and raised their weapons. But Lavaria just shook her head, realizing how foolish that had sounded. The team of fake knights was about to charge the over-sized Black Knight when suddenly, the Black Knight's whole body sizzled with an electric current. He raised his broadsword and blasted the five imposter knights backward. Jestro's crew flew through the air, splatting against and sticking to the front wall of the fake Fortrex.

"Uh," Moltor moaned. "Didn't expect that!"

"Are we ... moving?" Sparkks—who was disguised as Aaron—asked.

The Fortrex began to roll backward down the huge hill that led up to Hightop. First, it rolled slowly, but quickly picked up speed as it flew down the hill. "You *did* put on the parking brake, didn't you?" Lavaria squeaked.

Moltor held on for dear life as the rolling castle plummeted toward the bottom of the hill. "*What* parking brake?"

At the top of the hill, the Black Knight watched without expression while the fake Fortrex rolled away into the distance. The villagers of Hightop cheered, grateful to the mysterious Black Knight who had saved their village from destruction . . . for now.

CHAPTER 5

Nearby, the real Fortrex was hastily rolling away from the village of Pieburg. Once again, the knights had gone to visit the town with good intentions—but were quickly chased away by angry townsfolk. Standing atop the castle's front parapet, the five real knights ducked as villagers lobbed food and trash at them.

"Has everyone in this kingdom turned on us?" Clay yelled out. He ducked just in time to avoid a piece of pie hitting him in the face. It flew over his head and splatted against the castle's stone wall instead.

"I don't know," Macy said sadly. "But I think

we need protection from the people we're supposed to protect!"

Lance folded over, clutching his stomach as if he was going to be ill. He sobbed, "Gasp! What is happening to me? Am I dying?" He breathed quickly, in and out, letting panic set in. "This feeling! I have never felt it before!"

Aaron felt bad for his fellow knight, but also kind of liked that Lance had to taste a slice of humble pie. "It's called 'being unpopular,'" he told him.

"What?" Lance screeched. "You mean . . . this is what it feels like when no one likes you?" He folded over and continued to sob.

Suddenly, a full-sized pie came whizzing through the air. Axl reached one of his meaty paws into the air and grabbed it as it flew past. He happily gulped it down, then said, "Mmm . . . I love the angry Village of Pieburg!"

The knights raced into the Fortrex's

command room, eager to talk to Merlok 2.0 to see if the wizard knew what was happening around the Realm.

"Merlok, have you learned any more information about these strange attacks we're being blamed for?" Macy asked, addressing their leader's bright orange hologram form.

Merlok 2.0 seemed to be fading in and out of focus more than usual. It was almost as though his circuit was shorting or losing signal. "No," the wizard said. "But I've experienced an unusual amount of activity in my systems. It's made me quite itchy." The wizardly hologram scratched an ear, then his armpit, and leaned down to itch his foot.

"Uh," Clay said, averting his eyes. "Maybe you just need to shower. Or, uh, de-frag or something."

"Perhaps," Merlok 2.0 said, lifting his staff over one shoulder to get at an itch on his back. The orange hologram wiggled and wobbled as Merlok 2.0 struggled to fight the itch spreading across his whole body. "I contacted Ava at the Academy and she thinks someone might be 'hacking' into my system."

Clay and Macy exchanged a look. "We need to get back to the Knights' Academy, and have Robin and Ava run some diagnostics."

"Yes—diagnostics," Merlok 2.0 said, scratching even more violently. The poor wizard just couldn't seem to hit the right spot. "And perhaps a little digital flea powder!"

While the real knights made their way toward the capital to collect Ava and Robin from school, Jestro's team of imposter knights was headed for yet another town in the Realm. They were looking forward to a fun afternoon of looting and pillaging and making those goody-goody knights look bad.

"We've had a minor setback," Lavaria told the others as she scanned the forest around their vehicle. She and the rest of Jestro's team were gathered atop the fake Fortrex, plotting their next move after their failed raid in Hightop. "But we should be fine now. My spies tell me those other 'knights' are returning to the capital."

"Leaving the entire kingdom to us!" Moltor chuckled.

Moltor, Lavaria, and the others transformed from their black-and-red forms into perfect replicas of the knights once again, just as the Fortrex screeched to a stop. The five imposter knights tumbled to the edge of the Fortrex tower wall and peered down to the ground below. They were dismayed to see that they hadn't stopped because they had reached a village—but because the Black Knight was once again blocking their way.

"None shall pass," boomed the Black Knight.

Moltor rolled his eyes. "Ugh. Not him again. Can't we just run him over?"

Lavaria shook her head. "Not without damaging the 'castle.' And Jestro wouldn't like that."

"Okay, fine," Moltor grumbled. "But I'm not doing all that happy-knighty talky-talking again. This time, we just surround him—and finish him!"

The five evil knights charged out of the castle, ready to storm the Black Knight. But before they could strike, the Black Knight lifted his shield and began to flicker with energy. He lifted his sword and the blade opened into a five-bladed fan sword! The hulking Black Knight swung the new weapon through the air, sending each of the five imposter knights flying in all directions.

Behind the Black Knight, a crowd of villagers cheered. The Black Knight had saved the day once again.

But Jestro's team wasn't discouraged. Hours later, the fake Fortrex rolled up to another village in the Realm. The imposter knights charged out of the castle . . . and came face-to-face with the Black Knight *again*! "None shall pass," the knight announced.

Lavaria, Moltor, and the others stormed out of the Fortrex. Moltor made a fist as they surrounded the Black Knight, promising, "This time, we finish him *for sure*!"

But the Black Knight wasn't going down without a lot more fight. He lifted his shield, pointing it at the five knights. Suddenly, a huge metal fist popped out of the shield and blasted the bad guys out of the way, one by one.

Before long, Jestro's gang was fed up with the Black Knight. Every time they pulled up to a new town, they found that the giant protector was once again standing in their way. The next time they came to the edge of a town, the giant Black Knight was positioned in front of a grove of trees, blocking the road.

Atop the castle tower, Moltor growled, "Enough of this. I don't care if we damage this castle. We're running over that Black Knight!"

The Fortrex rumbled slowly forward, toward the Black Knight. Just as the castle was about to crush him, flames shot out of the bottom of the mech's boots. The force blasted the Black Knight into the air, sending him up and over the Fortrex. The Fortrex continued to roll full steam ahead.

"Ha!" Moltor cheered. "So much for those jet boots! We rolled right past him and—*ahhhh!*" Lavaria, Moltor, and the others all screamed as the Fortrex rolled right off the edge of a cliff and plummeted down to a rocky chasm below.

The Black Knight landed gracefully and safely on the cliff's edge. Beneath the steely helmet, the mysterious knight inside all that tough mech armor was smiling.

CHAPTER 6

Late that night, Jestro's team rolled up to its base camp in the middle of the forest, bumping and thumping and creaking along. The Evil Mobile could barely roll forward after its little spill over the cliff earlier in the day. It kept blinking and sputtering, looking like the Fortrex one moment . . . and the Evil Mobile the next. The thing was wrecked.

Jestro stood up to greet his team, eager to hear how the destruction was coming along. But when he got a good look at the vehicle and his mess of a crew, Jestro's face morphed into anger. "What happened?"

"Black Knight," Moltor said feebly.

"What are you talking about?" Jestro screeched. "We have the ultimate Powers of Deception! We can trick anyone. How did this so-called Black Knight beat you?"

Lavaria hung her head. "He tricked us."

"What?!" The Book of Monsters yelled. "What are you talking about?"

"To be fair," Moltor began. "We were trying to run him over. But we ran over a cliff instead."

"There was a lot of falling," Flama said.

"And landing," Burnzie added.

All the other monsters nodded their agreement.

The Book of Monsters sighed. "Look, here's what we do . . ."

"Silence!" Jestro screamed, interrupting The Book of Monsters. "No tricky Black Knight can trick Jestro the Deceptonator!" He paused, appreciating his new word. "I just made that up . . . pretty good, huh?" He glanced at the rest of his crew for approval.

Then he lifted his staff in the air and cried, "We shall fix this castle!"

The Book of Monsters cackled. "It's *deceptively* easy . . ." He sent his magical energy toward the Evil Mobile, transforming it back into the Fortrex again. A little magic made it look shiny, polished, and good as new.

Jestro grinned. "And this time, I shall personally lead you into battle against this so-called Black Knight!"

While Jestro and his crew made plans to defeat the Black Knight, Ava and Merlok 2.0 were hard at work on plans of their own. Ava punched at the computer in the real Fortrex's command room. She whipped her head around, glaring at Merlok 2.0 as she said, "It's really hard to type with you looking over my shoulder . . . even virtually."

"What are you doing?" Merlok 2.0 asked. Ava had been hard at work on something all afternoon, but she wasn't giving any of the knights any clues about what she was up to.

Suddenly, Ava gasped. "Ah! There it is!"

"There what is?" Merlok 2.0 wondered.

She pointed at the screen on the wall. An image of the Black Knight filled the screen. "The source of the hacking signal. We've got to head there now!"

Across the Realm, Jestro and his monster henchmen pulled up in front of the Black Knight—ready for one last fight.

"None shall pass!" the Black Knight screamed again.

This time, when the drawbridge on the fake Fortrex rolled open, Jestro and The Book of Monsters stepped out first.

"Jestro?!" The Black Knight gasped.

Jestro gestured to his team of "knights" and ordered: "Destroy him, please."

As the five imposter knights stormed toward the Black Knight, the giant mech lifted his sword, waiting for a weapon download. But this time, nothing happened.

The Black Knight glanced down at the signal bars on his shield, watching with horror as they went from full strength to no signal. "Impossible," the Black Knight whispered. "Someone's jamming my signal."

Before the knight could figure out how to fix his signal and weapons, Jestro's crew hit him with everything they had. Though the Black Knight was larger, the mech found it difficult to fight back against so many attackers at once. "Stop," he begged the knights. "Why are you doing this? You knights should be the heroes of the Realm . . . not Jestro's jerkies!"

But the "knights" would not stop. They continued to lob weapons and shots at the Black Knight, driving him backward.

Jestro giggled as he watched the battle, then turned to The Book of Monsters. "Got any more tricks up your book sleeves?" he asked.

The Book of Monsters grinned. "I've always got somethin' . . ." The magical book glowed and pulsed with energy. A moment later, a cloud of purple smoke appeared behind the Black Knight. *Poof!* A chest had appeared out of thin air.

"Whoa!" the Black Knight said, spinning around to inspect the outside of the chest. It was decorated with pictures of incredible weapons. "A chest full of weapons? Just what I need!" He reached forward and popped open the lid. But when the chest flew open, the Black Knight didn't find weapons inside . . . he found a horde of cruel, glowing Globlins and Globlin spiders! The tiny round beasts chattered and attacked, smothering the Black Knight as the fake knights continued their assault.

"Ha!" The Book of Monsters said with an evil smile. "Another deception! How fun is this?"

The Black Knight was soon brought to the

ground by the force of the angry mob of Globlins. They overpowered the knight, pulling at his mech to keep him from fighting back.

The Black Knight struggled to stand upright again, but the gang of Globlins pulled down hard. With a mighty *pop!* the Black Knight's mechanical arm was ripped off. The Knight looked at his shoulder, which was smoking and sizzling with frayed wires. "It's just a mech wound," he said, trying to reassure himself.

Furious, the Black Knight lifted himself to his feet—but the Globlins began to pull at his other arm. When the Black Knight tried to shake them away, the Globlins tugged the other mechanical arm right out of its socket. The Black Knight groaned. It was hard to fight with no arms . . .

"Now step aside, Black Knight . . ." Jestro ordered. "While you still have legs!"

"Never!" roared the Black Knight. He surged forward, then fell—*boom!*—to the ground. His legs were gone, and the enormous mech was now nothing more than a torso wobbling on rocky ground.

"Ha!" the Black Knight called, feigning confidence. "I'm just getting started. Think you've won? Well, I'll show you!"

But Jestro's team of "knights" and Globlins once again overpowered the Black Knight. It was soon clear there was no hope. "Okay," Jestro said, shrugging. "We'll call it a tie." Then the evil jester turned to his team of minions and ordered, "Now . . . please see who is inside this mechanical mess!"

CHAPTER 7

The imposter knights began pounding at the Black Knight's outer shell, trying to break through. But before they succeeded, the real Fortrex rolled into the clearing and the true knights came charging forward!

"Step aside, villains," Clay yelled. "We are the *real* knights of the land, sworn protectors of the Realm!"

"Uh," Moltor said. He glared at the real Clay, staring him down from across the clearing. "Nope, sorry. *We* are the knights of this Realm."

"No, you're not," insisted Clay. "We fight for justice! Courage! Chivalry!"

58

"So do we," blurted Moltor. "Juicebox! Curry! Shiver-me-timbers!"

"Huh?" Clay asked.

"*Blah-blah-blah!*" Moltor screamed. The rest of the fake knights echoed him and charged at the real knights, hollering, "*Blah-blah-blah!*"

But there was one thing the real knights had that the fake knights didn't.

"Prepare for NEXO Scan!" Merlok 2.0 said.

The knights quickly held up their shields.

"NEXOOO KNIGHTS!" Clay shouted.

"NEXO Power: Avenging Ultra Armor," Merlok 2.0 said.

There was a flash of light as the NEXO Power downloaded into their shields. The real knights glowed with their charged up armor and weapons. Clay was now armed with propellers, Lance with two big wings, Aaron with four green lasers, Macy with a huge cannon, and Axl with a pair of huge arms and fists on his back! They raced forward, ready to take the other knights down.

"What is all this talk of 'blah-blah-blah'?" Clay asked as he swung his sword at Moltor, who was still disguised as Clay. "I *never* say that!" He blasted Moltor so hard that the imposter went flying.

Aaron whipped through the air on his hover shield, going after his own doppelgänger. "Dude, you are sooo extreme—extremely lame, that is!" He blasted the fake Aaron.

Macy taunted Lavaria, saying, "Oh, c'mon . . . is that the best you can do?"

Lavaria growled. She swung hard at Macy, but Macy nailed her with a powerful jolt of NEXO Power.

Axl and Burnzie—who was disguised as the fake Axl—battled nearby. Burnzie leaned forward and sniffed Axl, curling his mouth into a sneer. "Eww, what'd you eat before?"

"Bacon-wrapped pork fritters," Axl said, licking his lips. "Why do you ask? Does my breath *stink*?" He let out a long exhale of pork-scented breath, blowing it straight into Burnzie's face.

Overwhelmed by the smell, Burnzie stumbled backward—and fell straight into the empty weapons chest. The lid slammed closed, and a horde of Globlins grabbed the chest and ran off with it.

"Ahh," Axl said with a belch. "Good food—and bad breath—save the day again! Yeah!"

There was one last imposter to take care of . . . the other Lance. But the real Lance was having some trouble disposing of such a magnificent-looking fellow. "How could I *ever* strike someone so handsome and stylish?" he asked, gazing at the mirror image of himself. Fake Lance whacked the real knight in the gut with his weapon. Lance looked up and swooned. "And so forceful, too! I dare say . . . you are the perfect man."

Imposter Lance swung at Lance again, knocking him sideways. Just as it looked like the bad guy was going to take him, Clay raced forward and slammed the last of Jestro's monsters aside with his sword. Having been defeated, each of the monsters magically transformed back into their original forms and fled. They scurried into the Fortrex for cover, which—*poof!*—turned back into the Evil Mobile once again.

"Brilliant!" Jestro cheered. "We have *deceived* them into thinking they have won, right?" He turned to The Book of Monsters— but found that his sidekick had already escaped to the safety of their vehicle. The Evil Mobile began to roll away. Jestro jumped and ran after it. "Hey! Wait for me!"

The Book of Monsters smirked, watching as Jestro raced to catch up to the others. "He's deceptively quick for a guy in a jester outfit."

"Come back!" the Black Knight shouted after Jestro and his team of monsters. "This isn't over. I can still bite you!"

But the villains were gone. The only people who remained in the clearing were the five *real* knights, Ava, and the Black Knight.

"Watch his arms and legs," Clay warned. The knights stepped aside as the Black Knight's disconnected arms and legs crawled and hopped around on the ground.

"Thank you, brave knights," the Black Knight said gratefully. "But how did you find me?"

Ava stepped forward, holding a tracking gadget. "Oh, it was easy," she said. "We just tracked down the signal of whoever was hacking our system—and then jammed the 'illegal' downloads!"

"*You* did that?" the Black Knight asked, incredulous.

Ava shrugged. "I can't take all the credit. Robin's the master mechanic, but we couldn't find him anywhere. So I had to make do with some gear I grabbed from his room."

"Well, you should have logged off the disable protocol first!" the Black Knight said.

Clay narrowed his eyes at the enormous mech, wondering how he knew so much about Merlok 2.0's digi-magic system. "Who *is* this Black Knight anyway?" he asked.

The Black Knight's suit of armor opened . . . and Robin popped out!

"Robin?" Ava gasped.

Robin stood proudly inside the pilot compartment of the battered Black Knight torso, gripping the controls tightly. He waved awkwardly. "Hey, guys. What's goin' on?"

"*You're* the Black Knight?" Clay asked.

Robin grinned. "I, uh, meant to tell everyone, but it seemed like you knights had gone bad. So I didn't know who to trust. I thought this Black Knight mech was the only way to beat you guys . . . who weren't really *you guys*."

Clay and the other knights exchanged impressed looks. "Nice work, lil' grommet dude," said Aaron.

"Thanks!" Robin said, flushing with pride. "So, uh, *now* can I skip school and go with you on all your cool quests? Can I, huh? *Can I, can I, can I?*"

Robin got his answer not long afterward, when the knights dumped him on the front steps of the Knights' Academy for the second time in less than a week. "Figures," Robin said, sighing. "They'll *never* take us with them."

He and Ava trudged into school, both feeling proud that they had helped save the Realm from Jestro's crew. But they were also both disappointed. They knew their lessons at the Academy were important, but it just seemed like they learned even more when they were out in the world with the rest of the NEXO KNIGHTS team!

As they passed a video monitor in the main hall, the screen blazed to life. Merlok 2.0's bright orange face grinned out at them from inside the video screen.

"Merlok?" Ava said. "What are you doing here?"

"Promoting you . . ." Merlok 2.0 said. ". . . to the next level of the Academy!"

"What?!" Robin asked, cheering.

"You have demonstrated excellence in technology," Merlok 2.0 said, nodding to Ava. Then he turned to Robin and added, "And you, in combat." He smiled serenely at both of them and added, "More than enough knightly skills to fulfill your requirements for this semester."

"Really?" Robin said happily. He began to jump up and down excitedly. "So no more Academy?"

Merlok 2.0 shook his head. "Well, not until next year. There is still much schoolwork ahead, and both studying and doing are important. But there is a time for studying and a time for doing."

"See?" Robin gloated. "Told ya I'm a doer!"

"Er, yes," Merlok 2.0 agreed. He glanced over his shoulder. "And I was also wondering

if you could help our knights 'do' a little . . .
uh . . . 'body building'?"

Behind Merlok, the knights were hard at
work on their next quest: reassembling the
broken Black Knight mech. "Are you *sure*
that's where the head goes?" Macy snapped
as Clay tried to stuff the headpiece into one
of the shoulder sockets. Then Macy and the
others tried to prop the mech up on its feet . . .
but the poor thing just fell to pieces again.

Robin and Ava both cringed. It wasn't easy
watching the noble knights look so helpless.
But the fact was: They were knights, not
builders. Robin knew that building things
was best left to the experts . . . like him. As
they made their way toward the doors that
would take them away from the Knights'
Academy for the rest of semester, both of
the knights' apprentices began to laugh.

They knew the knights were lucky Robin
and Ava would be helping out around the

Fortrex even more from now on. Thanks to Ava's brilliant tech skills and Robin's knack for building stuff, the knights could focus on what they were best at: protecting the people of the Realm. And with Jestro and The Book of Monsters still roaming around out in the world, there were sure to be plenty more heroic missions in store for the NEXO KNIGHTS heroes!

When it came time to face them again, the heroes would be ready . . . all seven of them.